Mr. Nobody

written by Pam Holden
illustrated by Pauline Whimp

1

Early one morning, Mom heard a crack like a whip!
She found a hole through the bathroom window.
"Look at these pieces of broken glass on the floor!
Who threw a ball near the window?" she asked
the three children.

2

"Not me. I didn't throw a ball," answered James.
"It wasn't me," said Molly. "I was reading my book."
"I was just playing with my doll," said Elizabeth.
"Oh, I see," said Mom. "I think it must have been
Mr. Nobody."

3

At lunchtime, Dad heard a splashing sound. When he came into the kitchen, he found milk spilled all over the table. It was dripping down onto the floor.
"Who made that mess with the milk?" asked Dad.
"Somebody should clean up the table and the floor."

4

Molly answered quickly, "I didn't do it, Dad."
"It wasn't me," said James. "I was sitting still."
"I was just eating my lunch," said Elizabeth.
"Well, it must have been Mr. Nobody again,"
said Dad. "There isn't anybody else here."

Later that afternoon, there was a bang like thunder.
The front door slammed shut with a loud crash.
"What a noise! Who slammed that door?" asked Dad.

6

Molly said, "It wasn't me. I was talking to Grandma on the phone."
"I don't know anything about it," said James.
Elizabeth said, "I didn't go through the front door."
"It must have been that Mr. Nobody again," said Dad.
"Who else could it have been?"

Just before dinner, Mom picked a big bowl of ripe
strawberries from the garden. The children thought
they looked delicious.
"Yum! We're having strawberries for dinner tonight,"
they said to each other.
"No, the strawberries aren't for you three," said Mom
and Dad together. "These are for somebody else."

"But we love strawberries," said the children.
"We could all share them. Who else could they
all be for? Can't we have some, please?"
"No, there aren't any for you today," said Mom and
Dad. "These are all for Mr. Nobody."
The children looked at the bowl full of delicious
strawberries, and then they looked at each other.

10

"Well, it might have been me who broke the bathroom window," said James in a quiet voice. "I'm very sorry. It was an accident. I must have hit the ball too hard with my bat. I won't hit any balls near windows again."

Elizabeth said, "I think I spilled the milk. I'm really sorry. It was an accident. I must have knocked it over, but I'll try to be more careful at the table."

13

"Well, I think I might have slammed the front door whe[n]
I was hurrying to answer the phone," said Molly sadly.
"I'm sorry, Dad. I'll go more slowly next time."

"We're really sorry," said all the children together.
"We'll be more careful next time."

Mom looked at the three sad faces and she smiled.
"Well, I don't think Mr. Nobody is still here," she said
to Dad. "So I guess everyone could share these delicious
strawberries after all."